THE
WISHING DOLL

Badger Publishing Limited, Oldmedow Road, Hardwick Industrial Estate, King's Lynn PE30 4.
Telephone: 01438 791037

www.badgerlearning.co.uk

THE
WISHING DOLL

BEVERLY SANFORD

Badger
LEARNING

The Wishing Doll ISBN 978-1-78147-967-4

Text © Beverly Sanford 2014
Complete work © Badger Publishing Limited 2014

Publisher: Susan Ross
Senior Editor: Danny Pearson
Publishing Assistant: Claire Morgan
Copyeditor: Cheryl Lanyon
Designer: Bigtop Design Ltd

2 4 6 8 10 9 7 5 3 1

CHAPTER 1

TWINS

"Just let me do it my way, Jae!"

Mia yanked the hairbrush from her sister's hand and stomped back to her side of the bedroom. Staring into the mirror, she brushed her hair into a neat ponytail and tied it with a band.

An identical set of brown eyes met hers in the mirror.

"I was only trying to help," said Jae. "Your hair looks really pretty in plaits."

No, thought Mia. *You just wanted everything your own way, as usual!*

"I like it in a ponytail," she said, picking up her school bag.

As she walked to the door, Jae touched her on the arm. "Are you cross with me? I don't like it when we fall out. Give me a hug… pleeease?"

Mia melted. She couldn't stay angry with her little sister for long. They were too close to become enemies. Only nine minutes separated the twins in age, although sometimes Mia felt like it was more like nine years.

She hugged Jae tightly, then sniffed as she smelled something familiar. "Is that my new body spray?"

"Sorry!" Jae said. "I didn't think you'd mind if I used it." She skipped off downstairs, humming.

Mia sighed. "No," she said, "you never do."

*

As Mia walked into the kitchen, Mum handed her her lunch. "Here you go. Ham and tomato rolls, just as you wanted."

"I asked for *cheese* and tomato," said Mia in dismay. "Jae wanted ham!"

"Oh, sorry love," Mum said. "But you usually have the same. It's too late to change it now."

"I'm not eating meat any more, remember?" Mia said, but Mum had already bustled out of the room with a pile of ironing.

"Mind you come straight to Nan's after netball, girls. Loads to do!" she called behind her.

"Hurry up, Mia!" yelled Jae from the hall.

Mia grumbled under her breath and stomped outside, but Jae was already out of the door.

*

"GO JAE!" cheered Hannah, the team captain, as Jae put the ball perfectly through the netball hoop. "She's so fast!" she said to Mia who was playing in defence.

"Yeah..." Mia nodded as Jae jumped up and down with joy.

"I heard Mrs Wood tell Jae to try out for the county team," Hannah said. "How about you?"

"Actually, I'm thinking of leaving the squad," Mia said.

"You can't leave!" said Hannah. "We need you."

"What?" Jae shrieked, overhearing them. "Leave? Since when? You didn't tell me!"

"Well I don't have to tell you everything!" snapped Mia. She marched towards the changing rooms, leaving Jae behind, bewildered.

*

"Look at these old photos!" Mum said, holding up a faded black-and-white picture. "There's Nan when she was about your age." She pointed at a teenage girl with the same long, black hair as the twins, frowning against a background of lush, green trees and busy fishermen.

"Trip to Lake Tai," Jae read aloud from the back. "Cool, this one's from China!"

Mia was still fed up. She and Jae had hardly spoken all the way to Nan's house and Mum was too busy to notice that something was wrong. "I know we need to clear it out for the new owners," she kept saying, "but your nan would be so sad to see her things getting chucked away like rubbish."

Mia hated seeing Nan's things disappearing one by one. Nan had died a year before and Mia still missed her every day. Nan had never treated the twins like they were the same person – she never gave them identical presents, like everyone else did, and she never mixed them up. "I always know which one is which!" she'd tell anyone who asked. "Jae is the one with a twinkle in her eyes, while Mia's are full of dreams."

Mum and Jae were poring over the photos. Mia felt too warm so she wandered out into the garden to get some fresh air. She loved the rainbow colours of Nan's flowers, and the pretty ornaments, like the birdbath with insects painted on it. The garden was huge – Mia loved getting lost in it.

Walking along the path, she caught sight of the shed. She'd never liked it much. Tucked away at the back of the garden in the dark among the trees, it was musty and full of cobwebs. There was never any room inside as it was filled to bursting with broken flowerpots and rusty tools.

Mia stopped to look at the roses, but a rumble of thunder made her jump. Suddenly, freezing hailstones pelted down, fast and furious.

"Argh!" shrieked Mia, icy stones slapping against

her school shirt. She turned to run back to the house, but remembered Jae. Spinning back around, she saw that the shed door was open a crack. She rushed inside.

Ducking under a huge cobweb, Mia squeezed the water out of her ponytail and wiped her face dry. Then a gust of wind shook the shed, rattling the window and sending pots flying. As Mia went to set a pot upright, the wind howled like a wolf.

CRASH! Something flew along the shelf and hit the floor. Then, just as suddenly as it had arrived, the wind died down.

Mia bent down to see what had fallen – a tin box, filthy but with tiny, blue flowers still peeking through on the lid. The impact had thrown it open.

Mia picked up the box and there, nestled inside, was the strangest doll she had ever seen. Small and delicate, clothed in a once-beautiful dress, it had painted features – dark eyes and a red rosebud mouth. But it wasn't smiling.

"You look sad, too," Mia whispered to it.

The doll stared back at her.

BANG! Suddenly the door burst open!

CHAPTER 2

THE DOLL

"What are you doing in here by yourself?" asked Jae, crashing inside the shed. "What's that?" She snatched the doll out of Mia's hand. "Eww! It's filthy!"

"Give it back!" Mia tried to snatch it back. "It's mine. I found it."

"It's horrible. Its face is scary!" Jae held it away from her.

Mia lunged at her. "Well give it back then!" She grabbed the doll but Jae hung on. "Jae! Give it back NOW!" She pulled hard, making Jae stumble against some boxes.

Jae immediately let go, looking surprised. "I was only looking. You didn't need to shout!"

Mia hugged the doll to her chest. "Sorry," she mumbled.

Mum appeared in the doorway. "What's going on? I can hear you from the house!"

"I made Mia jump. Just mucking about!" Jae said.

"Well stop winding each other up," said Mum. "What's that, Mia?"

Mia held up the doll. She didn't want to hand it over, it felt warm and close.

"It was in here," said Jae. She showed Mum the box.

"So that's where it went!" exclaimed Mum. "I thought Nan had got rid of it years ago."

"Have you seen it before?" asked Mia.

"Yes, it's from Nan's village. She wouldn't let me play with it when I was little, she said it was magic and it brought bad luck." Mum frowned.

Mia looked down at the doll. It still seemed sad.

"I wonder why it was out here," said Jae.

"Probably an accident," said Mum. "You know how she moved things about."

Mia wondered if Nan had forgotten about it. She'd gradually forgotten most things. She never seemed to forget Mia and Jae though. "I know your face," she'd say, whenever they visited. Suddenly Mia missed Nan more than ever.

Mum put her arm around her. "Have it if you want," she said.

Mia looked at the doll. "I'd like that," she said.

"Good," said Mum. "Right – let's get some dinner." She started back up the path, Jae following. Mia stood quietly with the doll, lost in thought.

*

"Just listen to this!" Jae shrieked. Mia dropped her fork with a clatter.

"'Sneaked out to the pictures with Jimmy Weir. Mum says he's a rascal but, oh, he's got such lovely eyes! He's so dreamy!'" Jae bubbled with laughter, getting louder and louder, echoing in the half-empty lounge. "A rascal! How funny is that?"

Mum rubbed her head. "I'm getting a headache."

Jae closed Nan's old diary with a snap and tapped her fingers on it.

Mia stared at her in annoyance. *Why is she so selfish?* she thought. *She knows Mum's stressed out.*

"So, how was netball?" asked Mum.

"Great! Mrs Wood thinks I'm good enough for

the county team!" said Jae.

"What about you, Mia?" asked Mum.

"She's dropping out!" said Jae before Mia could speak.

"What? You love netball," Mum said.

"I haven't decided yet," said Mia. She began to collect their plates.

"Well you need to decide soon!" called Jae, as Mia went into the kitchen.

I wish you would just shut up! thought Mia, dumping the plates in the sink. *Just stop talking for once!* She turned on the taps and sighed as a cloud of scented bubbles flew into the air. When the sink was full, she started washing up.

"Aaaaaaiiiiieeee!" The scream came from the garden.

Mia ran outside to find Jae clutching her mouth

"Mia will come with me, won't you Mia?" Jae turned her sparkling smile on Mia. "You'll look after me?"

"But I was going to work on my Art project!" said Mia.

"Oh Mia, please!" said Jae. "I really want to get my dress while the sale is on."

Mia gave in. "OK," she said. "But I don't want to be out all day."

"Yay!" Jae beamed at her. "Can I go then, Mum?"

"OK. But you come straight home if you feel ill," said Mum.

"Thanks!" whispered Jae as Mum left the room. She hopped over to Mia's bed and hugged her, then recoiled. "Ugh! You brought that doll home!" It was sitting upright on Mia's bed, staring coldly forwards.

Mia pulled it close to her. "You knew I was having it." She stroked the doll's head.

"It creeps me out," said Jae. "There's something weird about it."

"She's not weird. I like her!" Mia held the doll tightly.

"Why did Nan put it in the shed then? Maybe it's haunted!"

"Don't be stupid, Jae. Dolls can't be haunted!"

"Yes they can! By evil spirits. I saw it in a horror film."

"She's not evil. She just needed a home, that's all."

Jae sighed. "Fine! I don't want to fight about it. But does it have to be on your bed? It keeps staring at me!"

Mia looked at the doll. Its gaze was fixed on nothing, its stare blank. "She's not looking at anything. Don't be silly."

"Please Mia," said Jae. "Can't you put it in the cupboard?"

"Maybe." Mia smoothed the doll's dress.

"You're the best, big sister!" Jae beamed. "I'm calling first dibs on the shower!" She skipped out of the room.

As soon as she had gone, Mia held up the doll. "As if I'd put you in a cupboard!" she whispered. "You'd be so lonely." She put it in her bag and zipped it shut. "I promise you won't ever be left on your own again."

In the bag, the doll's lips curled just a fraction.

CHAPTER 3

JEALOUSY

"This one!" screeched Jae, turning heads and making Mia wince. She stepped back as Jae whirled to face the mirror, holding a purple dress.

"Yeah, try that one!" said Hannah. She and Jae went into the changing room in a huddle, clutching their dresses.

Mia looked through the racks. The dresses weren't her style, but Jae had insisted on looking in the town's biggest shop. Mia thought their clothes were too trendy.

Suddenly, someone bumped into her and she dropped the dress she was holding. She turned and saw a gorgeous older boy with dark hair and sparkling green eyes. He gave her a sheepish smile.

"Sorry!" he said. "My fault!" He picked up the dress.

Mia's heart pounded. "Umm… it's OK," she said. She felt her cheeks grow warm.

"Nice dress!" said the boy, looking at it.

Mia blushed harder. "Thanks," she eventually managed to say. "It's for my school dance."

"Cool. I'm looking for one for my dance, too!" joked the boy. Mia giggled.

Just then, a blond boy came over. "There you are! Come on Kris, we're going." He smiled at Mia. "Alright?"

Mia nodded, her cheeks on fire.

Kris laughed. "Alright, I'm coming." He handed Mia the dress. "Nice meeting you. You should get this!"

Mia's heart skipped about as he walked away. He was gorgeous! She wished she'd been brave enough to ask for his number – Jae would have done. *Maybe I'll see him again,* she thought.

Then she remembered the doll.

She opened her bag and took out the doll. "Umm... Hi," she whispered. "I don't know if you made that wasp sting Jae. But could I please ask for a wish?"

The doll stared back at her, eyes dark.

"Kris – that boy I just met? I wish I could see him again. Boys never like me but I think he did. So please can you help me? Thanks." She kissed the doll and tucked it into her bag just as Jae and Hannah came back.

"I'm getting this purple one," Jae announced. "It's amazing! Can we get lunch now? I'm starving."

"I haven't chosen anything yet," said Mia.

"We can come back after," said Jae. She walked off without waiting for an answer.

"Didn't like the dresses in here anyway," snapped Mia to nobody in particular.

*

"Ugh, what is that?" said Hannah, lifting the bun off Mia's burger. "It looks like dry mud!"

"It's a veggie burger," said Mia. "It's nice. Want a bite? It's – "

Jae butted in. "The boys had better make an effort to dress up for the dance, too."

Mia rolled her eyes.

Hannah laughed. "Anyone in particular? Like... you know... Tommy?" She smirked at Mia.

"Maybe," said Jae. "I dunno. The boys in our school are so immature. I wish I could meet someone older!"

Mia smiled. Kris was much cooler than the boys she knew.

Just then, a group of boys tumbled into the café. Mia's heart leaped into her mouth when she saw a flash of green eyes and a big smile – Kris! Her wish had really worked! She patted the doll inside the bag. *Thank you!* she thought.

"Look!" hissed Hannah. "Jae – your wish worked!"

Jae fluffed up her hair. "Think I'll wish to win the lottery next!"

Mia ignored Jae. She was too excited about seeing Kris again!

"One of them's looking over!" said Jae.

Mia looked at the boys and her heart sank. Kris was looking over – but he was looking at Jae!

"OMG he's gorgeous!" whispered Jae.

Mia tried to speak but couldn't get the words out. She couldn't believe this was happening! She had to make sure Kris saw her!

She stood up, knocking her drink over. Hannah caught it just in time. "Careful!"

"What are you doing?" said Jae.

Mia ignored her. She stood still, waiting for Kris to see her.

"Mia!" hissed Jae, tugging on her arm.

Kris walked towards their table, still smiling at Jae. As he got closer, he caught sight of Mia and did a double-take. He looked from her to Jae, confused. Then he laughed.

"There's two of you!" he said. "So who did I meet earlier?"

"Huh?" said Jae. She shot Mia a confused look.

"That was me. Mia," said Mia. "Jae, I met Kris when you were in the changing rooms."

"You didn't tell me," said Jae, her eyes as big as saucers. "You usually tell me everything!"

"You were in a hurry," said Mia.

"Must be fate!" laughed Kris. "But, wow – twins! That's pretty cool."

Jae gave him her most charming smile, then patted the seat next to her. "I'm Jae, by the way. Want to join us?"

*

Mia was fuming! Jae was stealing Kris right before her eyes. From the minute he'd sat down, she'd taken over the conversation and made it all about her. Even worse, Kris was falling for it.

"How can people tell you apart?" he asked, smiling at Jae.

"Well…" Mia began, but Jae jumped in.

"That's easy! Mia's the geek. She's always wearing one of her billion zillion *Doctor Who* T-shirts, like she is now!"

Mia could practically see Kris losing interest in her on the spot.

"Cool…" he said. "I'm not really into that stuff. I'm more into sports."

"Me too," said Jae. "I'm going to be on the county netball team, actually."

"That's great," Kris said, looking impressed.

"You should check out one of our games," Jae flirted.

"Maybe I will," flirted Kris right back.

At that moment, Mia hated her twin.

She grabbed her bag and squeezed out of the booth. Jae and Kris didn't even notice.

"You OK?" whispered Hannah.

"I met him first," Mia said. "It was me that he met." The tears threatened to spill down her cheeks, so she blinked furiously.

"Oh," Hannah said. "Maybe you should tell Jae. She'd hate to upset you."

"Yet she always does," snapped Mia. She stomped off to the bathroom and shut herself in a cubicle. Taking out the doll, she stared deep into its eyes. "This isn't what was supposed to happen!" she said. "Did I do something wrong?"

The doll stared back at her.

"He was mine," Mia said, sniffing back tears. "He wasn't meant to fancy her. She's not right for him – I am. I wish he'd just stop fancying her."

Was it her imagination, or did the doll's lips turn up the tiniest bit?

Mia shook her head. What was she thinking? It wasn't a magic doll. There were no such things! It was just coincidence, that's all. Jae had been stung because the wasp had gone in her drink. And the café was near the clothes shop, so it was no wonder Kris had turned up there. Just coincidences.

She put the doll away and wiped her eyes. It was just a doll. It couldn't really make wishes come true, could it?

Then she heard Jae screaming at the top of her lungs.

CHAPTER 4

BAD WISHES

Racing outside, Mia saw Jae flailing her arms around, crying. Kris stood back, looking horrified.

"What's wrong?" called Mia, rushing to her sister's side.

"We don't know!" said Hannah. "It just happened!"

"What just happened?" asked Mia, trying to see Jae's face, which she was covering with her hands.

"No, don't look! It's awful!" wailed Jae, clutching her face so tightly that her knuckles went white.

"Let me see!" said Mia firmly. She prised Jae's fingers away and gasped in shock. Jae's whole face, from forehead to chin, was covered in angry, purple spots.

"They just appeared out of nowhere," said Kris.

"Maybe it's from the wasp sting," said Hannah.

"Yeah… maybe," said Mia, feeling a guilty blush creep up. "I need to get her home." She put her arm around Jae. "Mum'll sort it out, don't worry."

She called Mum to come and get them. Then she waited, one arm around Jae, the other clutching the bag with the doll lurking inside.

*

"They're going down," said Mum, dotting cream on Jae's face. "But I don't think the sting caused it. What else did you do today?"

"We tried on clothes and had lunch," Mia said.

"Oh, wait – Jae tested some make-up."

"Jae!" wailed Mum. "What am I always telling you? Don't try on testers! You know how sensitive your skin is."

"It was only powder," sulked Jae, glaring daggers at Mia.

"Well it looks like you've had an allergic reaction to it," said Mum. "Not helped by the one you had to the sting. Now, rest!"

She tutted and left the room.

"Thanks a lot!" snapped Jae.

"Well she needed to know!" snapped Mia back.

For the rest of the evening, the girls shared their room in sullen silence. Jae lay on her bed with her back to Mia, headphones clamped on. Mia lay on her bed reading. Her emotions jumped from fury at Jae's behaviour with Kris, to guilt at what had happened to her. She kept casting glances at her bag – it felt like the doll's stare was burning through it.

At least I got her away from Kris! she thought.

The silence was broken by Jae squealing in delight. Mia kept her back turned even though she was curious.

"Mia! Guess what?"

Mia ignored her.

"Mia! Oi! Come on, don't be like that. I'm not cross any more. Guess what?"

Mia sighed and turned round. Jae was standing up, smiling and waving her phone about.

"You know that boy from earlier? Kris? He got my number from Hannah!" Jae was beaming. "He's texted to ask how I am. Can you believe it?"

Mia couldn't.

Jae carried on. "I thought the spots had put him off but he's been so sweet. He says they'll look good with my purple dress! Anyway, we're meeting up when I'm better. Isn't that amazing?"

Mia said nothing.

Jae stared at her. "Aren't you pleased for me?" Her face fell. "Did you like him? He's not right for you. You need someone more like you."

Mia couldn't stand it any more. She stood up and put her hands on her hips, facing off against Jae. "And just what does that mean, exactly? 'More like me'?"

Jae backed up, looking alarmed. "What's the matter with you? Why are you being all weird and angry?"

"Because I'm fed up with you!" Mia yelled. "You're so selfish all the time!"

Jae's eyes widened, then she burst into tears. "Why are you being so mean? I've had a really horrible few days."

"Poor little Jae!" snapped Mia. "Well guess what? Some of us have had a horrible life being your twin!" She knew she was being awful and cruel, but she couldn't help it. It was like someone had opened the floodgates.

"Don't say that!" sobbed Jae.

"You know what, Jae? I wish I'd never had a sister!" The words were out of Mia's mouth before she could take them back.

Suddenly the room began to spin. It span until Mia felt too dizzy to stand. She gasped and staggered backwards to her bed.

And then the room went black.

CHAPTER 5

SISTERS

When Mia awoke, it was morning. The sunlight streamed through the windows as she prised her eyes open. She felt groggy, like she hadn't slept well. She shook her head, trying to remember the strange dream she'd been having. Then suddenly she remembered – Jae!

She turned over and gasped in shock. Jae had gone! And so had all her things – even the bed!

"No!" she cried. "This can't be happening!"

Jumping out of bed, she ran around the room trying to find some small trace of her twin. She searched in the wardrobe, the drawers – even looked for Jae's beloved cuddly toys on the shelf – but there was nothing. The room was different – as if her own things had stretched and filled out the space, rather than being squeezed in with Jae's.

"No, no, no!" howled Mia, crumpling into a heap on the carpet. "I want my sister!"

She heard voices from downstairs. "Jae!" cried Mia, jumping to her feet.

She ran down the stairs, following the sound of voices into the kitchen. Mum and Dad were cooking breakfast and chatting. But Jae wasn't there.

"Morning, love!" said Mum, catching sight of her in the doorway. "Want a cuppa?"

"In a minute," said Mia breathlessly. She ran out of the room and into the living room – Jae wasn't there. Mia rushed to the mantelpiece where Mum kept family photos. Jae was missing from all of them! But her netball trophy was still there. Mia spun it around. "'Player of the tournament – Mia Green'," she read aloud. "Oh no!" she sobbed, putting her head in her hands.

"What on earth's wrong?" Mum had followed her in.

"Where's Jae?" Mia asked.

"What?" said Mum.

"My sister – my twin!" wept Mia. "Tell me where she is!"

Mum's face clouded over. "You know how much that upsets me. Why bring it up?"

"What? Do you know where she is? Why isn't she here?" Mia grabbed Mum's arm in desperation.

Mum shook her off. "You know what happened. She was taken from us before she was even born. Honestly Mia, why would you be so cruel?" She walked away, upset.

Mia stood still, totally shell-shocked. "This is my fault," she whispered. "I wished for this to happen!"

Then she remembered the doll.

She ran back upstairs and pulled the doll out of her bag. It was freezing cold and its eyes were like black ice.

"Please bring her back!" she begged it. "I didn't mean it! I unwish it!" She shook the doll hard. "Do you hear me? I UNWISH IT! Just bring her back!" Then she put it down and crept under her covers to cry.

*

The day passed by in a dream. Mia couldn't concentrate on anything. Several times she begged the doll for help, but nothing changed. Jae remained gone.

Later that day, Dad popped his head around her door. "I've just picked up some stuff from Nan's.

Thought you might like these." He put a bag down. "I'll call you when dinner's ready."

Mia waited until he'd gone before opening the bag. Inside were the diaries that Jae had been looking at, the ones Nan had written when she was their age. She began flipping through them – some entries were about Nan missing her home village in China, and a lot were about school and boys. *Just like Jae!* thought Mia, with a pang. Suddenly, an entry caught her eye.

What have I done? I knew that doll was evil!

I should have put it away where it couldn't harm anyone. It's all my fault!

"Oh!" gasped Mia. "Maybe there's something in here that can save Jae!"

She flipped back through the pages and her heart filled with fear as she discovered Nan's terrible secret. The doll *was* magic – a wishing doll from her village. It was said to bring good luck to its owner… unless it was used for a bad wish.

Evil spirits are always looking for bad wishes. They are drawn to them like moths to a flame. And once they find them, they look for somewhere to take root; a home.

Nan had wished for something very bad indeed. And that something had found her.

"Oh Nan," sobbed Mia as she read on.

I hate her so much! Why should Irene be chosen for the swimming team and not me? I'm so sick of her. She's always picked for everything! I just wanted Dad to be proud of me for once. Well, I'll soon show her! I'll get my doll to make sure Irene Wilkins is off the team once and for all!

The doll had done exactly as she had wished. Poor Irene had drowned in an accident. Not long after that, Nan had been given her place on the team.

Chills crept across Mia's spine. She felt as if eyes were burning into the back of her head. Turning, she saw the doll peering out of her bag. She felt sure it knew what she was reading!

She read more, hoping Nan had left a clue about how to stop the doll. Eventually, she found it. Just one entry, the last one Nan had ever made.

It's too late for Irene, but maybe I can still do some good. If you're reading this and you have the doll, please – don't use it. Don't let it take your wishes! Su-Lin said a good deed will always fight a bad one. But I think the only way to stop it is to make a deal with the evil spirit. A sacrifice to restore the good and banish the bad.

Mia turned the pages but there was nothing else. "Is that it?" she yelled. "What does that even mean?" She studied the words again and again. Then she turned to the doll. Its eyes were alive, mocking her.

"Whatever you are – whatever is in there, please hear me. I made a mistake. I made the wrong wish. Please, please will you bring Jae back? Whatever it is you want – whatever the sacrifice I must make, I'll do it. I'll do anything! Just bring her back."

Mia held the doll tightly and she waited, whispering quietly to it over and over again, "Bring her back. Please. Just bring her back."

And the doll began to work.

CHAPTER 6

SACRIFICE

"Help me! Please, someone help me!"

Mum rushed into the bedroom and found her daughter tossing and turning, crying out in distress. She shook her awake, cuddling her close.

"It's OK darling, I'm here. You're safe. Did you have that nightmare again?"

"It was horrible, Mum. So dark and scary. I didn't know where I was. I was so lonely!"

"It was just a bad dream. Dreams can't hurt you."

"I'm so glad you're here, Mum. But sometimes I wish I had a sister to share things with – I bet I wouldn't have nightmares then."

Mum smiled sadly. "I wish you did, too. But here, look, you've got Nan's doll to keep you company. She'll look after you." She picked it up from the nightstand and put it on the bed.

Jae hugged it. "You're like my sister, aren't you, doll? Did Nan have a name for it?"

Mum paused in the doorway. "I don't think so. Maybe you can give her a name."

"I know just what I'll call you," said Jae. "Mia. I'll call you Mia."

The doll's rosebud lips curled in a sad little smile.

THE END